Straight
from the
Horse's
Mouth!

published by

National Center for Youth Issues

Practical Guidance Resources
Educators Can Trust

ncyi.org

www.ncyi.org

From the Horse's Mouth! is warmly brought to you by the horses and humans at Take Flight Farms. We dedicate this book to those who believe that horses have the power to heal and to our clients whose courageous journeys are an inspiration to all of us.

A VERY special thank you to
The Dick and Helen Kelley Family Foundation
for their kindness and generosity.
Thank you for making this book a reality.

Duplication and Copyright

P.O. Box 22185 • Chattanooga, TN 37422-2185
423.899.5714 • 800.477.8277 • fax: 423.899.4547
www.ncyi.org

ISBN: 978-1-937870-12-6
© 2012 National Center for Youth Issues, Chattanooga, TN
All rights reserved.

Written by: Julia Cook • Illustrations by: Allison Valentine
Design by: Phillip W. Rodgers • Contributing Editor: Beth Spencer Rabon
Published by National Center for Youth Issues • Softcover
Printed at RR Donnelley • Reynosa, Tamaulipas, Mexico • November 2012

My name is
Archie.

I am a horse…
but not just any
horse. I have a real
important job. I
help people get rid
of their flies. You
know, the things
that bug us.

When horses get flies, we just swish our tails
and make them go away. But since people
don't have tails, they come to me for help.

When people are having a tough time with life,
when they can't seem to tell what is wrong and what's right.

They come here to see me, and even those who have doubts,
are just blown away when they figure things out.

I am a horse, and horses can help people fix ANYTHING!
You see, horses have something that people don't have…

horse sense!

About 10 sunups ago, a sad girl came to see me. She had a lot of flies bugging her. I could tell just by the way she walked that her insides were sore. I think she had barbed wire stuck inside of her, and she needed to get it out of her body. She had tried cutting holes in her skin to let the barbed wire out, but it must not have worked.

At first she ignored me, and I ignored her.
She acted like she'd been mistreated.

But then she could tell I knew just how she felt,
'cause I know what it's like to feel cheated.

*I knew if I kept doing just what horses do,
she'd see it's not all about her.*

*I made her be the one to come up to me first.
It took courage and strength for sure!*

*When she reached out to me, I reached out
right back, and her flies seemed to go away.*

*When the girl learned how to believe in herself,
her whole world changed that day!*

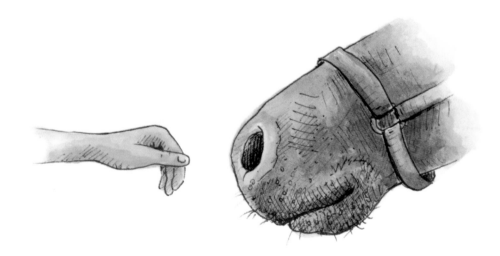

When people with flies come to see me, my **horse sense** tells
me what I need to do. Some people need to be ignored at first,
and others need my closest attention right away.

I've been working with a very strong boy now for quite a few sunups. When he first came to see me, he was way out of control. He had a lot of flies, and he was doing everything he could to make them go away.

I once heard a man tell the strong boy to "stop horsing around!" Humans have absolutely NO idea how offensive that phrase is to a horse! Maybe I should start saying,

"Stop humaning around!"

When the strong boy first came here, he put up a front.
He was reckless and angry and full of "I won't!"

So I started to act exactly like him.
I was his mirror…when he'd smile, I'd grin.

When he tried to act scary, I'd do that too.
When he ran, I would run. I knew just what to do.

Then one day while leading me, he took off my rope.
I continued to follow him…because I had hope.
The boy was amazed that I'd followed his lead.
At that very moment, I met one of his needs.

When the boy jumped over a human toy,
I did the same, and his eyes filled with joy!
He started to see that he had what it took
to be a leader in life, with a positive look.

He also figured out that the way that he acts,
makes a difference to others, when they look at him back.
At first when he came here, he was out of control,
but now he's a leader, and he's starting to grow.

One time, not too many sunups ago, a nice girl came into the arena with a bunch of boys. Even though the nice girl was with the boys, I could tell that on the inside, she was all alone. She had a ton of flies!

The nice girl walked away from me, and stood by the fence. She had lots going on, and I could feel she was tense.

When she looked down at the dirt, I saw pain in her eyes. Then the dirt turned to mud, because she started to cry.

When I walked over by her, the nice girl walked away.
The last thing she wanted was me by her that day.

But I followed her anyway, because that's what she needed.
Her flies tried to take her trust, and they had succeeded.

I know what it feels like to be all alone,
when your trust turns to heartbreak, and your hope is all gone.

The rest of the world may have quit on this girl,
but horses aren't quitters, I know that for sure!

So I nudged the nice girl, so she'd know I was there.
Then she motioned to me, "Hey! Get out of my hair!"

Then the girl walked away again, so I started to follow.
I would not give up on her, even though she felt hollow.

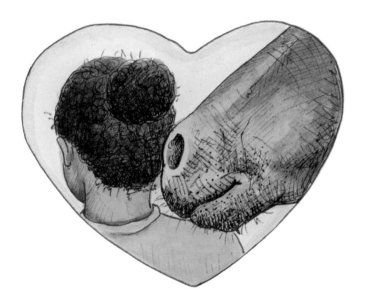

At first the girl thought I was being a pest,
but I didn't care, I kept trying my best.

By the end of our session, I knew she had grown,
when she whispered to me, "I don't feel so alone."

guilt

disconnect

Yesterday, a soldier came to
spend some time with me.
He walked with a limp and
carried a stick with a bent end.
He had a lot of flies.

uncertainty

shame

defeat

loss of
Control

I looked at the soldier, and I knew in my heart,
he limped on the inside and was falling apart.

He just couldn't handle who he had become.
Life as he knew it, was pretty much done.

regret

I stood tall, and I looked at him right in the eye.
I could tell in a minute, he was all out of "try."

anger

It hurt him to stand there, I could tell by his sway,
so I laid down in the dirt, so he'd know it's ok.

He sat there beside me and played with my mane.
What the soldier did not know, is that we were the same.

Before I came here to live at this place,
I was one of the best in every horse race.

Then one day my life changed, and now here I am.
So I totally get why this guy's in a jam.

The soldier didn't say much,
but he didn't have to.

I knew exactly what he was
going through.

Near the end of the session, the soldier took paint,
and wrote all his flies on the side of my flank.

The soldier had given me all of his flies.
Now without them, I knew he'd be able to try.

When I rose to my feet, his eyes saw my scar.
Then he whispered to me, "I know who you are!"

I raced into the pasture as he opened the gate.
What brought us together sure must have been fate.

With his flies on my back,
I raced into the field.

Now the soldier had hope
and a chance to rebuild.

Like I said before, my name is Archie and I'm a horse with an important job! I help people get rid of their flies. Since I have good horse sense, I'm really good at what I do.

So the next time you have flies, stop **"humaning around,"** and go spend some time with a horse!

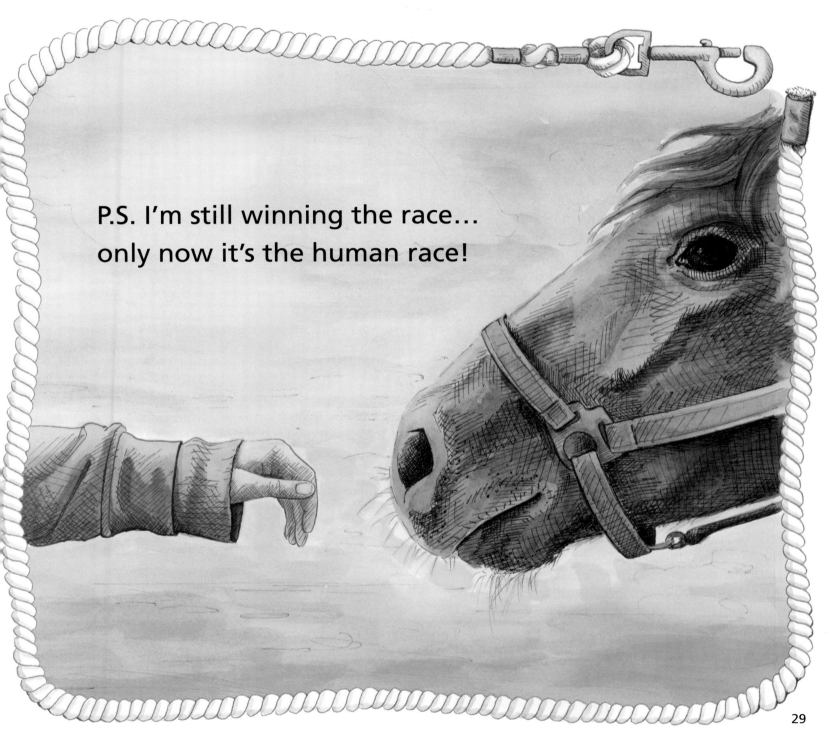

P.S. I'm still winning the race…
only now it's the human race!

Take Flight Farms

Where Horses Make a Difference

About Take Flight Farms

Take Flight Farms, a nonprofit organization based in Omaha, Nebraska, holds the "Distinguished Program Member" status within The Equine Assisted Growth and Learning Association (EAGALA). Take Flight's highly trained Licensed Mental Health Professionals and Equine Specialists work with their clients in creative horse-centered activities designed to address specific treatment, learning or educational goals. Take Flight addresses a variety of mental health and human development needs including behavioral issues, substance abuse, trauma, depression, grief, eating disorders, abuse, anxiety, relationship problems, resiliency and communication challenges. This specialized work done on equal footing with the horse (no riding is involved) allows participants to explore, experience, discover, problem-solve and overcome challenges. Take Flight works with numerous agencies, schools, hospitals, military programs, families, and individuals of all ages from diverse backgrounds.

To learn more about Take Flight Farms, visit **www.takeflightfarms.org**.

Meet Archie!

Archie was born on a cattle ranch in Western Nebraska, and was named after his owner. When he grew up, he was given an important job – he worked the cattle on the ranch, moving them from place to place. One day, Archie found himself in a metal building on the ranch during a very bad storm. The building blew down with Archie inside. He ended up getting a very bad wound on his foot that would not heal. Since Archie couldn't work, the rancher gave him away. But the people who took him didn't really want him, so they gave him to other people who didn't feed him very well.

One day, a very kind lady saw Archie in a pasture and rescued him. He lived at her house and found lots of love and wonderful pastures to graze in, but he seemed lonely because he was the only horse in the pasture. So, his wonderful lady brought him to a horse farm where he currently lives today. Now Archie gets to play with lots of other horses. Archie's lady still comes to see him, and she gives him lots of love and carrots.

Archie now has a new important job. He works at Take Flight Farms helping humans figure out how to heal on the inside. Archie understands what it feels like to be hurt, hungry, and lonely. Now, he is given unconditional love, a full stomach, a safe forever home, and lots of other horses and humans to hang out with.

About EAGALA

There is a growing interest in incorporating horses to help youth, adults, families and groups address emotional, mental and behavioral health needs. This is known as Equine Assisted Psychotherapy and Equine Assisted Learning.

This form of therapy is especially helpful, as the horses provide an emotionally safe way to project strong and difficult feelings stemming from life's traumas and challenges.

Founded in 1999, EAGALA is the leading international nonprofit association for professionals using equine therapy to address mental health and human development needs. EAGALA provides training and certification in Equine Assisted Psychotherapy and Equine Assisted Learning. All EAGALA Model sessions use a team approach consisting of a Licensed Mental Health Professional and an Equine Specialist. All activities are ground-based. No riding is involved - rather the horses respond to the clients naturally and become metaphors for other relationships and issues in life. Sessions are solution-oriented, and programs must abide by EAGALA's high standards and code of ethics.

You can learn more about programs in your area through EAGALA - the Equine Assisted Growth and Learning Association - at www.eagala.org.

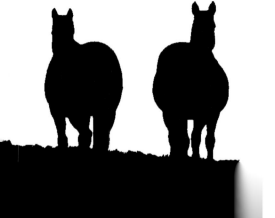

Coming Soon!

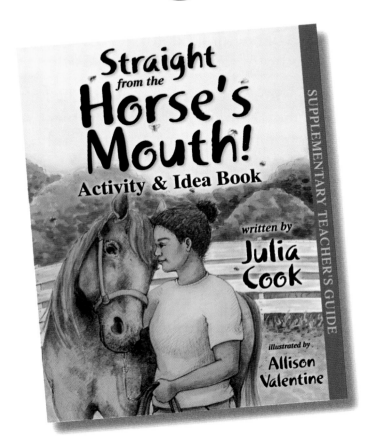

Straight from the Horse's Mouth!
Activity & Idea Book

SUPPLEMENTARY TEACHER'S GUIDE

written by Julia Cook

illustrated by Allison Valentine

Great for Counselors, Teachers, and Parents!

National Center for Youth Issues
Practical Guidance Resources
Educators Can Trust

ncyi.org

www.ncyi.org